W9-CCC-629

For our grandparents—
Gertie & her "sweet W.J." and Jimmy & his "Georgia Mae."
Thank you for fighting the tide. And for the old boat.

Copyright © 2021 by Jarrett Pumphrey and Jerome Pumphrey

All rights reserved
Printed in the United States of America
First Edition

For information about permission to reproduce selections from this book, write to
Permissions, W. W. Norton & Company, Inc., 500 Fifth Avenue, New York, NY 10110

For information about special discounts for bulk purchases, please contact
W. W. Norton Special Sales at specialsales@wwnorton.com or 800-233-4830

Manufacturing by Worzalla
Book design by Aram Kim
Production manager: Julia Druskin

Library of Congress Cataloging-in-Publication Data

Names: Pumphrey, Jarrett, author. | Pumphrey, Jerome, author.
Title: The old boat / Jarrett Pumphrey, Jerome Pumphrey.
Description: First edition. | New York, NY : Norton Young Readers, an imprint of W. W. Norton and Company, [2021] |
Audience: Ages 4-8. | Audience: Grades K-1. | Summary: "Off a small island, a boy and his grandfather set sail in their
beloved fishing boat. They ride the waves, catching wants and wishes and seeing the wonders of the ocean.
But soon the boy is sailing the boat himself, drifting further from shore as the waters grow muddied and turbulent.
When a storm washes him ashore, he sees home in a new light. He decides to turn the tides of his fortune, cleaning the
island's waters and creating a new life with a family to call his own"—Provided by publisher.
Identifiers: LCCN 2020008285 | ISBN 9781324005179 (hardcover) | ISBN 9781324005186 (epub) | ISBN 9781324005285 (Kindle edition)
Subjects: CYAC: Boats—Fiction. | Water pollution—Fiction. | African Americans—Fiction.
Classification: LCC PZ7.P97328 Oj 2021 | DDC [E]—dc23
LC record available at https://lccn.loc.gov/2020008285

W. W. Norton & Company, Inc., 500 Fifth Avenue, New York, N.Y. 10110
www.wwnorton.com

W. W. Norton & Company Ltd., 15 Carlisle Street, London W1D 3BS

2 3 4 5 6 7 8 9 0

Jarrett Pumphrey   **Jerome Pumphrey**

THE OLD BOAT

Norton Young Readers • An Imprint of W. W. Norton and Company
Independent Publishers Since 1923

Off a small island, an old boat rode the tide.

First shallow.

Then deep.

Then deeper.

The old boat caught wants

and wishes,

waves

and wonders.

But the old boat rode farther

and farther.

Far from home, the old boat was cold

and lonely

and lost.

On a small island, a new sailor turned the tide.

First shallow.

Then deep.

Then deeper.

Off a small island, an old boat was home.